AVENGERS

» AVENGERS: ASSEMBLE!

Written by
Tomas Palacios

Based on Marvel's
The Avengers
Motion Picture Written by
Joss Whedon

Illustrated by
Lee Garbett,
John Lucas, and
Lee Duhig

Based on
Marvel Comics'
The Avengers

ABDO Spotlight

MARVEL
NEW YORK

ABDOPUBLISHING.COM

Reinforced library bound edition published in 2018 by Spotlight, a division of ABDO, PO Box 398166, Minneapolis, Minnesota 55439. Spotlight produces high-quality reinforced library bound editions for schools and libraries. Published by Marvel Press, an imprint of Disney Book Group.

Printed in the United States of America, North Mankato, Minnesota.
042017
092017

www.marvel.com

THIS BOOK CONTAINS
RECYCLED MATERIALS

TM & © 2012 MARVEL & SUBS.

LIBRARY OF CONGRESS CATALOGING-IN-PUBLICATION DATA

This title was previously cataloged with the following information:

Palacios, Tomas.
Avengers : assemble! / written by Tomas Palacios ; based on Marvel's The Avengers motion picture written by Joss Whedon ; illustrated by Lee Garbett, John Lucas, and Lee Duhig.
   p. cm. -- (World of reading. Level 2)
MLCM 2012/42183 (P)
[E]--dc23
                    2011279236

978-1-5321-4059-4 (Reinforced Library Bound Edition)

ABDO

Spotlight
A Division of ABDO
abdopublishing.com

This is the story of the Avengers!

Meet Tony Stark.

He is very smart.

He likes to build things.

Tony built a suit of armor.

He is now called Iron Man!

Iron Man can fly!

This is Bruce Banner.

He is a scientist.

He works in a lab.

When Bruce gets angry,

he turns into the Hulk!

The Hulk is very big

and green!

Next is Thor.

He is from another world.

Thor has a magical hammer.

He can control lightning!

Thor has a brother.

His name is Loki.

Loki is a very sneaky villain.

Steve Rogers is small and weak.

He wants to be big and strong.

He wants to fight for what is right.

Later, he becomes

Captain America!

He fights for justice!

Cap has a shield.

It is red, white, and blue.

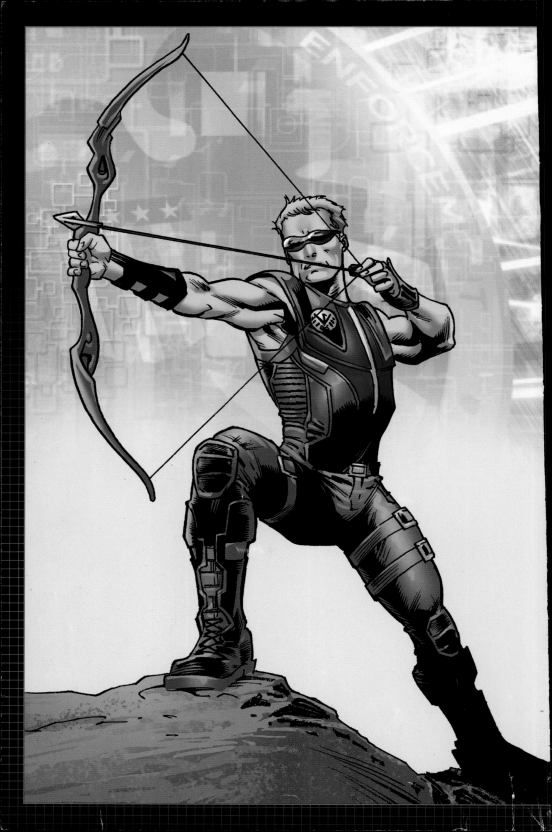

Next up is Clint Barton.

His code name is Hawkeye.

He uses a bow and arrow.

He is a great shot!

There is also

Natasha Romanoff.

She is called Black Widow.

She is a superspy

and a good fighter!

Finally, there is Nick Fury.

He is the leader of S.H.I.E.L.D.

S.H.I.E.L.D. is a special
group that helps people.
Nick Fury wants to make
a new group to assist
S.H.I.E.L.D.

Nick Fury creates

a team of Super Heroes.

He calls them the Avengers!

The Avengers fight for good.

They use their powers

to stop bad guys.

When there is trouble,

the Avengers assemble!